WINTER Wonderful

THE SUMMER UNPLUGGED SERIES

CHAPTER 1

The apartment I share with my husband has a whimsical glow inside now that I've decorated the living room with Christmas lights. I decorated the outside patio as well, but we never get to see those. It's entirely too cold to spend our evenings on the patio like we did in the summer. So I wanted to bring some holiday cheer inside.

Becca would call it my Christmas Cockles.

I have no idea what a cockle is, but she swears it's a real thing. Says her grandparents say it when someone is extremely in the holiday spirit.

Anyhow.

My cockles and I hang out in the living room while Jace uses his magic to slice up the pizza he just took out of the oven. I can never slice it in a remotely decent manner. All the pepperonis slide off and push the cheese all over the place and make a mess. At least, that's the excuse I used when I flashed him my angel eyes and asked him to do it for me.

"Now that we're almost parents, we probably shouldn't eat pizza like three nights a week," I say as I spin around the living room with my arms up, basking in the glow of the multi-colored lights. I had turned off the main light when Jace went into the kitchen. Now everything is shadowy and colorful.

Our Christmas tree, however, is not colorful. Jace likes the clear lights for trees, says it makes the tree look more beautiful that way. I tend to get my way with everything around here, so I let him have that, those silly clear lights, just to see him smile.

"Nonsense," Jace says, reaching up into the cabinet and taking out two plates. "Pizza has grains in the dough, tomatoes in the sauce and protein in the pepperonis. Oh, and dairy in the cheese. It's practically a perfect combination of the food pyramid."

I roll my eyes. "Well, when you look at it that way…"

He looks awfully proud of himself for coming

up with that elaborate excuse to make pizza seem healthy. He puts two slices on each plate and hands me one. "You still want water and not a delicious Coke?"

"Why do you have to say it like that?" I ask, placing a hand on my chest and making myself look terribly offended. "Of course I want water. I gave up caffeine months ago for our unborn son."

He gives me a sideways look to show me that he's skeptical. "I was just testing you."

"You're not going to catch me in a lie, *Mr. Adams*."

"Oh, you've done it now," he says, dropping his pizza and diving toward me. I cower into as much of a ball as I can fit my big pregnant self into and bury my head in my hands. It's no use though. Despite playing dead on my end, he still tickles me, right over my ribcage where I'm the most ticklish.

Jace still isn't over the event that happened at his work last week. While he was training a new client, a twelve-year-old boy, the kid thanked him and called him the worst name ever. *Mister*.

The kid had said "Thanks Mr. Adams" a million times, at least that's how Jace had explained it to me when he came home ranting and raving about how he is *not* old and he can't believe someone called him that.

So yeah, making fun of the more mature version of his name is my favorite pastime now. But now I'm dying from being tickled and it briefly occurs to me that it's weird how something that makes you laugh is also considered a form of torture. This. Freaking. Sucks.

"I'm sorry, I'm sorry!" I squeal as I try to writhe out of his fingers.

"I forgive you," he says. Finally, he relents and slides his hands up and down my arms, leaning in behind me to kiss my hair.

He's been doing that a lot lately—holding me by the arms instead of wrapping his hands around my stomach. Although he hasn't said anything about it, I'm pretty sure it's because I hate when anything draws attention to my big, huge, belly. So what if I'm nine months pregnant. It's still awkward and I hate waddling around all day. I hate the thought that I've gained weight more than just the baby. I have recurring nightmares that after he's born, I'll suddenly weigh five hundred pounds and Jace will hate me.

Maybe it's just the pregnancy hormones or whatever, but damn have I become a nightmare factory. My dreams focus on two topics: Jace leaving me or something terrible happening to our baby.

God I hope it's just the hormones.

I scarf down the pizza, telling myself it's just for now, just until the baby arrives and then I'll go back to eating healthier. Plus I'll have a child to run after and take care of and hopefully that will keep me active and help me get back into shape. We watch TV while cuddled on the couch and I let my mind wander into unfamiliar territory: motherhood.

I've been thinking a lot lately about how to be a mother. Sadly, just being pregnant teaches you absolutely nothing about raising a child. We have the crib and the stroller and the car seats. The tiny baby socks and enough clothing for the first year. We have a Great Wall of Diapers that lines one side of the hallway, thanks to a ridiculous diaper shower my best friend Becca had thrown for me a few months ago.

We had just returned from our honeymoon of traveling around in a private jet, and Becca surprised me with a handful of our friends and family (mostly people from the motocross track) and they all had diapers for us. Since I had gone on a little bit of a shopping spree myself, buying everything I'd need, there was really no point in having a traditional shower where people brought normal baby gifts. I had everything. Name it, I have it. If any baby store within a fifty feet radius had a baby product, you better believe I own it.

That's one of the things I love about Becca. She's smart in a way that surpasses other people's best friends. She knew I wouldn't want people giving me outfits and toys they had picked out simply because I'm so ridiculously picky about things, so she arranged a way for me to get exactly what I needed. I'm so glad she's dating Park now. After Jace had what can only be considered a fatherly talk with his best friend about how he better not hurt Becca and better treat her right, things got really good for those two. It's like Park realized what he had in a girl like Becca and he knew he didn't want to let her go.

So far he hasn't. And Jace would kill him if he did. At least...he'd try to. I'd kill him first.

My head rests on Jace's shoulder and I tuck my fingers underneath his upper arm, snuggling it to me as if his muscles were a pillow. It's Friday, the night before Christmas Eve, and Fridays are always a night where we stay up late and catch up on all the recorded shows we had missed during the week.

For some reason, I am incredibly tired tonight.

Jace is warm and his t-shirt is soft as I rest on it, closing my eyes. At some point I am aware of him leaning over and kissing the top of my head while his thumb runs back and forth over my knee. But then, I drift off to sleep.

THE TELEVISION IS STILL ON WHEN MY EYES OPEN. IT must not have been long because the same hour-long show is still playing on the TV. Jace is looking at his cell phone, clearing out all of his missed notifications.

I peer up at him and he gives me a smile. Then everything—everything—changes.

"Babe?" I ask through gritted teeth. "What's a contraction supposed to feel like?"

"You're asking me because I have all this vast personal knowledge of giving childbirth?"

I throw a couch pillow at him and rise to my feet. Without thinking, I start pacing the area right in front of the television. My thoughts are going a mile a minute. "It's just that in all those doctor visits we had, they told us to make sure to go to the hospital when the contractions are five minutes apart and all that, but they never told us what it actually feels like."

Jace cocks his head to the side and slides his phone back in his jeans pocket. "I'd imagine it's just really painful, like in the movies. Why are you asking that now?"

"Because," I say, but then the pain soars through my abdomen and I can't finish my sentence for a few seconds. "Because I think I'm having one right now."

CHAPTER 2

"Oh shit, oh shit." Jace grabs my wrists, stopping my pacing in front of the TV. His eyes go wide, almost hysterical in his excitement. "We're about to have a baby." He smiles. Like this is the greatest thing in the world. I glare at him. "What?" he asks.

I take in a deep breath and head toward the couch, wondering when the next contraction will come. It was painful, yes, but it was awkward and scary too. I'm not sure I can survive through more of these things. Jace joins me.

"Babe, why are you giving me that look?"

"Because you are not allowed to stand there and get all excited about a baby." I make air quotes when I say the last word. I put a hand on my stomach. "This thing is not even close to being here. I still have to suffer these contractions until they're five minutes apart and then we have to go to the hospital, and God knows how long labor will take, and what if there's an emergency and they have to rush me off and cut me open and—yeah, Jace. You don't get to be excited yet! This is terrifying!"

My husband's face is a mixture of emotions ranging from fear to worry to that stupid look of adoration that he usually gets when I'm yelling at him. I shake free from his grasp, grit my teeth and glare even harder at him.

He wraps his arms around me and pulls me into a big, pregnant hug, resting his chin on top of my head. "Everything that happens from here on out will become a part of the story we will tell Jett about the day he was born."

I swallow, focusing on my breathing. "You're right. I want it to be a good story." Not one where his mom is raging around being a crazy hormone monster and yelling at his dad. That's not the story anyone wants to hear. I draw in another slow breath and then release it.

I take my phone from the coffee table and open the timer app, starting it a couple minutes too late since I've already had one contraction.

Jace takes a step backward and holds my hands. "So what do we want to do while we wait?"

I look around our apartment, with it's beautiful glowing Christmas Cockles, three stockings hung up over the fireplace, and warm cozy blankets on the couch. I can't even lie—I've spent the last couple of weeks getting some serious television watching on while cuddling with my blankets. At nine months pregnant, there's really nothing else to do.

"I say we watch TV."

Jace plops down on the couch, extending his arm across the back of the cushions as an open invitation for me to come sit next to him. "Sounds good to me."

I take the remote and give him a sly smile. "But…I think this shouldn't be just any old TV watching day."

"What's that supposed to mean?"

I go to the DVR and find all the shows I've recorded to watch while Jace is at work because he hates them so much. "I think Jett would love to hear the story about the night he was born and how his daddy let his mommy watch all of her favorite shows because he loved her *so much* and he didn't mind one bit."

"Oh my God," Jace groans, throwing his head

back against the couch. "I walked right into that one, didn't I?"

My smirk is as big as my belly. I press play on my favorite reality show about a failing hair salon. "Yup."

"Six minutes and fifteen seconds," Jace says. He restarts the timer on my phone and rubs my back, because I guess it makes him think he's helping me feel better but he couldn't be more wrong. These contractions are the worst! No amount of back rubs will take away the pain that is searing through my lower abdomen, but I don't tell him that. I let him continue thinking he's being helpful.

"Should we go to the hospital now?"

I shake my head. "That's not even close to five minutes apart. It's been three hours…I think we're fine."

Jace frowns but he doesn't say anything. We've been watching reality shows for the last three hours and timing my contractions. They're slowly getting closer together but at this rate, it might take throughout the night, right? Anyway, I don't want to be in the hospital. I want to be home with Jace, not on an uncomfortable bed in a blindingly white sterile room full of strangers.

"Doctor Qi said five minutes. We're waiting until five minutes."

"But it takes twenty minutes to get to the hospital so we should leave slightly before they're five minutes apart that way when we get there it'll be exactly five minutes."

"I'm pretty sure my doctor calculated in the time to get to the hospital when he said five minutes."

Jace lets out a massive sigh and kisses the top of my hair again. He's been doing that a lot lately. I'm not sure if it's to make me feel better or to make himself feel better. Then it dawns on me that it's definitely the latter. Jace spends so much effort reassuring me anytime I'm upset about anything. He's always there. He's always been my rock, my place of loyalty. Jace doesn't freak out. Jace doesn't need help or comfort or reassurance.

Unless, maybe he does.

I untangle myself from the throw blankets and scoot closer to him on the couch. In the old days, before I was a whale, I could toss my feet over his, slide my arms around his neck and pull myself into his lap in about three seconds flat. It was effortless.

Now…that's a different story. I actually stand up first, lean over, and kind of fall into him. I'm not exactly in his lap, but I'm close.

Jace's arms go around me on instinct, but he's watching the TV with a zoned-out expression in his eyes. Faint creases stretch across his forehead, signs of stress on his otherwise gorgeous face. I take his head in my hands and turn him to where he's looking at me.

"Honey," I begin. This makes him snap out of whatever thoughts had been going through his head.

"What's wrong?" he asks, concern filling his eyes. I laugh on the inside. This is so like Jace. Always worried about me and never worried about himself.

"Honey," I say again, holding his cheeks in my hands as I look into his eyes. "We are about to have a baby and it's going to be awesome. You are going to be the greatest dad in the whole world, which won't mean anything compared to how great of a mom I will be, but that's beside the point. Everything's going to be fine and we're going to remember this night for the rest of our lives. I need you to stop worrying, honey. We've got this under control."

He takes my hand and kisses it. A smile softens the lines in his face. "You sure about that?"

I nod. "Women have been having babies for a bazillion years. In fact, the entire human race has been dependent on that very fact." Jace laughs and I lean forward and kiss him. "And that was before Doctor Qi and hospitals and all the fancy technology we have now. We're gonna be fine."

His head tilts to the side and he pulls me closer to him until I'm snuggled against his face. "Thanks," he murmurs into my ear. I hold onto him as if my life depends on it. I take in his smell, the woodsy scent of his cologne and the freshness of the clean shirt he put on after his shower. In these few seconds, everything feels calm and perfect. Somehow, my speech made me feel better, too. It's true, the whole women having babies thing. We will be fine.

It's still terrifying.

"Oh mother of hell," I screech between clenched teeth as another contraction pulls at my insides. It's very unsettling to have something going on in your body that you can't control.

Jace grabs the phone. "That was five minutes and three seconds. Please say we can go to the hospital now."

I nod through the pain and climb off of him. "Let me pee first," I say as I skip-run to the bathroom. The last thing I want is to pee all over myself in the middle of the highway during a bad contraction. Jace would probably never forgive me for doing that in his precious truck.

When I return, Jace has both of our Go Bags hauled over his shoulder and the TV is off and his truck keys are in his hand. Just seeing him like that gives me chills. "This is happening," I say with what I think is a smile on my face.

He nods and opens the front door. "Next time we're in this living room there will be another person with us."

CHAPTER 3

I've never been afraid of Jace's driving. And that's saying a lot because the guy has spent his entire life racing dirt bikes so reckless driving and speed are two of his greatest talents. But now, as we soar down Interstate 45 to the hospital, I find myself gripping the door handle and holding on for dear life.

"What are you doing?" he asks, glancing over quickly before gliding the truck into the left lane.

"Just praying to every God in the universe to please get us there safely."

I must have looked really scared because Jace lets off the gas and reaches over for my hand. "Sorry."

I glance at the speedometer and watch the orange needle fall from the high eighties into a more legal high seventies. Even though the speed limit is sixty-five. "We're not in that much of a rush babe."

"That's not what you said when you were having a contraction a few minutes ago," Jace says. I shrink back in embarrassment. I might have yelled a few expletives and demanded that he practically teleport me to the hospital right freaking now. But that was during a contraction. I am a different person in those few seconds.

When we reach the exit for the hospital, I let out another curse. Of course the exit is packed full of cars. "Who the hell is on the highway at eleven o'clock at night?" I snap. "Bunch of idiots!"

Jace laughs and slows to a crawl, eventually coming to a stop behind a row of cars that backs up from the upcoming red light. "Well it is a Friday and it's two days before Christmas. Last minute shopping, parties, stuff like that."

Oh God another contraction is happening. "Stop sticking up for these assholes," I say. "I hate every single car on this road right now. I hope all of them get coal in their stockings."

Jace puts his hand in mine and leaves the other one on the steering wheel. "Just squeeze my hand until it's over," he says. I do, and he doesn't even flinch.

After what feels like five thousand hours on the road, we pull into the parking lot of the hospital. "Should we go in the emergency room?" Jace asks. "Or just the regular entrance?"

"I don't know. Is this an emergency? I mean I'm not dying." Why didn't the doctor tell us this kind of stuff? Mentally I scan through all the baby prep books and the brochures I read in the waiting room at my OB-GYN. Nothing. Absolutely nothing. People should really tell you this kind of stuff.

"It's not that big of a hospital," I say. "Just park and we'll walk in the regular door since the elevators are right there." I do know one thing, and that's to go straight to the third floor. The maternity ward.

I have another contraction in the elevator but luckily we're the only two people in here so I get to make an ugly face of pain in front of the only person I will allow to see me looking ugly. When the doors ding open, we step out into a pastel colored hallway with a gigantic stork painted on the wall. I would give anything for the stork to be real right now. How wonderful would it be to have a creepy bird walk into our house and drop off our baby, no pain involved?

A fake Christmas tree sits in the corner, decorated in a half-ass kind of way with blue and pink ornaments and a few obviously fake presents placed underneath it. It's kind of weird to think that Christmas is just two days away. Well, one day, because I think it might be midnight already. Christmas is so far out of my radar because the only thing that's been on my mind for weeks is this baby.

We follow the arrow stickers on the floor that turn left and take us straight to the nurse station. Two nurses in scrubs sit behind the counter, both watching something on a tablet and commenting on how fat an actress has gotten this year. I clear my throat. One of them looks up and the other one touches the tablet to pause the video.

"Hi, how can I help you?" the first one says.

Um, seriously?

Who the hell asks a question like that?

Jace and I are standing here in our pajamas, Jace holding two big bags that are clearly packed with all the things we'll need during a hospital stay and I'm so pregnant I'm about to burst and we're standing right in the middle of the *maternity* ward…

"We're wondering if you could point us in the direction of the nearest amusement park," I say with a fake smile on my face. "I was hoping to go ride some roller coasters."

The woman doesn't seem to get my sarcasm.

"She's going into labor," Jace says. "Contractions are four and a half minutes apart."

"Oh!" She bursts into action as if, oh I don't know, it was her *job* or something. "This way," she says, guiding us into a delivery room. "Who's your doctor?"

"Doctor Qi from Mixon Medical," Jace answers. She gets me settled into a bed that's not totally as uncomfortable as I had feared and then leaves us while she gets everything else ready.

"Your sarcasm is on point lately," Jace muses. He sets the bags on a table and then sits on the edge of the bed. "I think pregnancy has made you exceptionally quick-witted."

I laugh. *"How can I help you?"* I say in a mocking voice. "I mean seriously? Who asks that to a pregnant woman in a maternity ward."

A little while later, the anesthesiologist comes into my room. He's a short Asian man with long black hair that's tied in a low ponytail. He's wearing dark blue scrubs, which is a drastic contrast to all the pastels that everyone else seems to be wearing. "Are we ready for your epidural, Mrs. Adams?"

I nod. Over the last few months of checkup appointments with my OB-GYN, I had heard a lot of women talking about pain management during labor. Some of them were staunchly against epidurals, claiming that natural childbirth is the way to go. Sure, it sounds heroic as hell to have a baby with no drugs, but sorry. I'm not that kind of person.

These contractions are killing me. I can't even fathom the pain of having a kid. Mom had told me there was nothing to be ashamed of. She'd had me with no drugs because they arrived at the hospital late and then with Bentley she'd opted for an epidural and said it was the greatest thing ever.

The anesthesiologist goes through a tray of medical supplies and tells me to sit up and swing my legs over the side of the bed. It occurs to me now that I have no idea what an epidural actually is.

"Um, what are you doing?" I ask, glancing back over my shoulder.

"I'll be inserting a needle into your spine," he says. "It doesn't take long."

"Oh holy shit." I swallow. A needle into my spine? Gross. I have about a thousand more questions but I'm not sure if I want to know the answers. Why did I have to send Jace on a snack run? He had to go all the way down to the cafeteria on the first floor so he might be gone forever. I need him here. There's about to be a needle in my freaking spine!

The doctor numbs the area first with a small needle prick. It's not so bad. He tries telling me every step of what he's doing but I ask him as politely as possible just to leave me in the dark about this. I really don't want to know. There's a slight knock on the door and Jace enters. I can't see him because my back is to him but I can tell it's him by the sound of the gasp he makes when he enters the door.

He nods hello to the doctor and joins me on the other side of the bed. He has sour gummy worms and pizza flavored pretzel snacks. My favorite. I smile at him and reach for his hand. He looks like he's seen a ghost.

"You okay?"

He does this half shrug half grimace thing. "I'm…I'm okay."

"What is it?" I ask.

"Hold still," the doctor says. I can feel his hands on my lower back but that's about it.

Jace swallows and the look of having eaten something rotten stays on his face. "I'll tell you in a minute," he says, closing his eyes.

"We're all done," the doctor says, closing the opening on the hospital gown I'm wearing. "You'll start to feel it soon. And congratulations on your baby," he says, patting me on the arm. Then he leaves the room and we're all alone again. Having babies in the movies always makes it seem like nurses and doctors are surrounding you all of the time. Here, I'm kind of left alone a lot.

I turn to Jace. "Are you getting sick?"

He shakes his head. "I'm okay now. I just…ugh. I walked in right when he was shoving a needle the length of my arm into your back. It was so gross. Wasn't that painful?"

"IT WAS THAT FREAKING LONG?" My eyes almost burst out of my skull.

Jace nods. "Pretty much."

Now I feel like throwing up. Although a nice warm sensation is slowly filling my lower body. I sigh. "It didn't hurt. He numbed it first."

"That's good. Babe you're the strongest person I know."

He was probably just being nice. In most cases in life, I am a total weenie. But his words fill my heart with happiness anyhow. I lie back on the hospital bed, resting my hands on my huge belly. Another contraction is coming on but I can't really feel it. Damn, this epidural thing works fast.

CHAPTER 4

Doctor Qi enters the delivery room, pulling a badge on a lanyard over his head as if he's been getting dressed on the walk over here. "Hello, hello," he says with the big smile he always has. "Looks like baby Jett just couldn't wait a few more hours until I've had my coffee."

I smile and Jace shakes his hand. I think it's so cool that my doctor remembers what we're naming our baby even though he has a ton of other patients. I wonder if he remembers those things about everyone.

By this time in my pregnancy, I am used to being poked and prodded by doctors and nurses so I don't even flinch when he puts my legs in the stirrups and starts feeling around in there. "You're nine centimeters dilated," he says. "He's almost here. Then I can get back to my coffee and start my day at a reasonable hour."

For a brief moment, I lose all the anxiety of childbirth and start getting really excited about it. Soon, I won't be a waddling whale of a person. I'll have my body back and I'll have an adorable baby to love and care for.

But then it's time to push and all that happiness had I felt vanishes just as quickly as it arrived.

The pushing is a nightmare. It's this weird feeling and even though I'm supposedly numb from the waist down, I've never been in more pain. And the doctor and nurses keep saying to *push harder* and I'm thinking *I am pushing harder!*

Jace is on my side, holding my hand and being the supportive, loving husband so well you'd think he'd spend his entire life prepping for this moment. I keep my eyes focused on him during what is so freaking awkward and weird and painful and surreal.

And then, somehow, and almost suddenly, the nurse hands me our baby.

CHAPTER 5

I don't know what I expected. It's embarrassing, really. The nurse puts a purplish-pink, kind of slimy baby on my chest and he cries and clenches his fists. The miracle of childbirth, right?

Yet the first thing that goes through my mind when I see my son is something along the lines of *oh my god this is a baby*.

Like really? Am I that stupid?

I mean, I knew there was a baby inside of me, I had seen the ultrasounds and watched him grow each week. But there's something to be said for seeing your baby in real life for the very first time. It's absolutely terrifying.

Suddenly it's all real.

All at once, as if those nine months of pregnancy were suddenly gone and they never happened. Now, officially, it's real.

He cries. It's a little baby cry and his face is scrunched up and his hands ball into fists that are so tiny…

And then I'm crying too.

CHAPTER 6

"Six pounds, ten ounces," the nurse says in a Spanish accent. She runs a careful thumb over his hair, which is a little auburn like mine and then fits a tiny little baby cap over his tiny little baby head.

"Congratulations Mr. and Mrs. Adams," Doctor Qi says. "You have a very healthy, very handsome little boy."

Jace shakes the doctor's hand. He crawls into bed next to me and kisses my sweaty, disgusting forehead. "I am convinced there is nothing you can't do," he says. For some reason this makes me blush. He's my husband and all, but he just watched me shove a baby out of my vagina, so yeah. Awkward.

Jett wriggles in my arms and it surprises me that I'm naturally holding onto him. That he's not falling out of my grasp or crying or demanding that someone with some talent take care of him. I mention that to Jace in a hushed voice so the nurse on the other side of the room won't hear.

"Are you kidding?" he whispers back as he gently strokes our son's chubby little cheek. "You're his mamma. He loves you more than anyone else in this world right now."

Just hearing those words from Jace fills my heart with some kind of atomic bomb sized emotions. "I love you, too," I whisper to Jett. Then, I add, "Jett. My sweet little Jett," because I'm not sure if he knows his own name yet.

"That's a pretty badass name," I tell Jace.

He nods. "Well, with me as a dad, he should expect everything in his life to be badass." I roll my eyes and wish I could punch him but I am so not about to move with my arms around this tiny little baby.

THEY MOVE US FROM THE DELIVERY ROOM INTO OUR own recovery room on the maternity ward. The walls are painted with a rainforest mural so there's all kinds of colorful animals watching us as we fawn over our baby. That's exactly what Jace I do. Fawn.

I sit up in bed, letting the back part of the bed rise up into a sitting position and then Jace sits at the foot of the bed and we let Jett lie all bundled up like a burrito between us. The nurse helped me breastfeed him which wasn't as scary as I had imagined and now he's sleeping.

"So, what a birthday." Jace looks at his watch. "He's probably going to hate it."

"Why's that?" I ask, looking up at him and then glancing at the time. It's four-thirty in the morning. "Oh wait… what day is it?"

"Christmas Eve."

My first thought is *how cute* but my second thought is, "Oh."

How had I forgotten what day it is? We're going to be in the freaking hospital on Christmas day. "Jett will just have to get two sets of presents," I say defiantly. "No child of mine is going to hate their birthday."

Jace laughs. "I knew you'd say that."

Our nurse knocks twice on the door and then opens it slowly, smiling at Jett as she enters the room. I assume she's here for vitals again but instead she says, "Would you like me to take him into the nursery now?"

"Huh?"

Jace says, "We can't keep him?"

"Oh of course you can," she says with her unfailing smile. "But most mothers like to take the baby to the nursery overnight so they can get some sleep. We'll bring him back at eight in the morning."

"Oh I'm not tired," I say just as my stupid body betrays me and makes me yawn.

Jace looks at me and then at Jett and then back at me again. "Honey I think we should let him go to the nursery. You do need some sleep."

I frown and pick up my baby burrito, kissing the top of his head. I don't want to let him go. He's mine. Why do they think I should let him go?

As if sensing my hesitation, the nurse says, "You can always keep him with you, that's no problem. But it's probably better if you get a good night's rest so you'll have energy to spend the day with him tomorrow."

Okay, that makes sense. Frowning again, I hand him over and watch her take him out of the door. There's a window next to the door so I can watch as she carries him to his little plastic crib thing in the nursery, the one that says ADAMS, J&B on the side of it. I assure myself that he's just a few feet away in the other room and that he's being cared for by an excellent team of nurses. But that doesn't help much because suddenly I am overwhelmed with sadness.

"I miss him already," I say to Jace.

"I know, baby but you need some sleep. You've been awake almost twenty-four hours." He lowers the bed's back into a flat position and then slides up next to me, resting on his side. I turn to face him and close my eyes when he runs his hand through my hair.

Okay, I think, as sleep overwhelms me. *Maybe I am tired.*

CHAPTER 7

I'm grateful for the sleep. Because at ten in the morning, visitor hours are officially open and everyone comes to see Jett. My mom, David and Bentley arrive promptly at ten, only I'm not sure who they are at first because all I see is a disembodied hand holding a dozen baby balloons walking toward me. Mom pokes her head out of them and I smile.

"My baby!" she says in a way that only moms can do as she throws her arms around my head, hugging me close to her. She smells like lavender and laundry detergent. "Now where's my other baby?"

Jace is sitting in the uncomfortable hospital recliner in the corner of our room, holding Jett in his baby blanket burrito. Turns out you're supposed to keep them all wrapped up like that for the first few days. (Apparently the baby burrito-style blanket wrap is a skill only the nurses possess because I still really, really suck at it.)

David takes the balloons and secures them to a table, then sets down a massive vase of flowers. "You guys didn't have to do that," I say about the flowers, but David just waves me off as it wasn't a big deal. He gives me a hug and I find myself thinking that I'm so glad Mom is happy now with a man who treats her right.

Bentley, who insists on being called Uncle Bentley now, completely bypasses telling me hello and heads straight for the baby. "Ahem." I clear my throat sarcastically. "Uncle Bentley better say hi to me or he won't get to hold his new nephew."

"Okay, okay," he says, trudging across the room and giving me a hug.

Even with my long night/early morning's sleep, I'm still tired. Jace handles showing Jett to my family and around noon, they decide to get some lunch from the hospital café. I take the opportunity to step out of my bed and waddle to the bathroom.

Only I'm not really waddling anymore and my steps are almost exactly like they used to be before my stomach got all fat.

I flip on the light to the little bathroom in our hospital room and sit down to pee. All I can see is my face in the mirror in front of me and I almost don't recognize myself. My hair looks like I've spent the day at the beach, when in reality, I just got really sweaty and then fell asleep without washing it. My face is pale and there's dark circles under my eyes. I make a mental note to remember how terrible I look so that I can thank Jace profusely later for putting up with me.

When I stand to wash my hands, something catches me off guard.

It's myself.

I stand straight, letting the water in the sink run as I stare at myself in the mirror. I'm wearing a massive t-shirt of Jace's and some flannel pajama bottoms. I don't really even remember changing out of my hospital gown last night but I think maybe Jace helped me.

The clothes aren't what's weird. It's my body that's weird.

I turn to the side and lift up my shirt, watching in awe at what's revealed in the mirror. I run my hand over my belly, which is now just a little soft and a little more protruded than it used to be. Wow.

I am almost completely the same size as before the pregnancy.

A little thrill of excitement courses through me and I want to jump up and down, but instead I just smile like a goofball at myself in the mirror. I wasn't a fat cow like I thought I was. I just had a baby inside of me.

Plus my boobs are still huge so that's kind of awesome.

I lower my shirt, giving myself one last smile in the mirror and then return to the hospital room.

Becca comes to visit a few minutes later, carrying a big balloon that's shaped like a little blue baby foot and another vase of flowers. They're sunflowers which I've decided in this very second are my favorite type of flower.

"Where's Bayleigh?" she asks, turning around right as I exit the bathroom. I crash into her, pulling her into a bear hug. "Wow, you're skinny!" she says, tapping my belly when I pull away from the hug.

"Thanks for coming," I say, and for some reason I'm almost in tears. She's my best friend, of course she would come. But this is a huge occasion and I'm just so excited to be sharing it with the people I love.

"Don't kid yourself, Bay," she says sarcastically. "I came here for my Jett not for you." She sticks her tongue out at me and then rushes over to Jett. Jace hands her the baby and then steps aside so she can sit in the recliner with him. She tells us that Jett is absolutely beautiful and even though I already know this fact, it turns out I can't get tired of hearing it.

Jace's phone beeps and he checks the text message. "I'll be back in a minute," he says, kissing the top of my head. I should probably really take a shower soon so he can stop kissing my unwashed face.

When he returns, Becca looks as happy as I do. His best friend Park is with him, looking a little disheveled from the flight he took from California to get here. He's holding a massive floral arrangement with a little blue teddy bear on top of it. "Congratulations, Bayleigh," he says, leaning over and giving me a quick hug. "These are for you."

"Thanks, Park. They're beautiful." I point him to the table against the wall so he can set the flowers down and he lets out a breath when he sees my other flowers. "Well then, I see my gift is not very original," he says with a smile.

Jace shakes his head. "Nah, man. She's obsessed with flowers. You did a good job."

I'm not sure I'd say I'm obsessed, but, I mean, seriously. You have no idea how much you'd love a room full of flowers until it happens to you and suddenly you're sitting in a room full of flowers that people brought just for you.

It is pretty awesome.

Park holds out his arms to get a hug from Becca and she looks so bashful when she leans into him. I swear that girl is so crazy in love and so crazy in general. Those two were meant for each other.

"So when are they letting you out of here?" Park asks when it's his turn to hold Jett. He makes these little goo-goo noises toward the baby and I'm pretty sure Park has never been around an infant in his entire life. Becca seems totally enraptured by the way he plays with Jett, though. Maybe she's thinking about having a baby herself.

That would be so freaking awesome to be best friends and have children the same age, but I know better than to say that out loud right now.

Jace tells him we're supposed to stay two days so we'll get out of the hospital the day after Christmas.

"Cool," Park says as he lets Jett wrap his tiny little hand around Park's pinky finger. "I'm guessing we'll cancel the Christmas party, or maybe just do something low key. Since our little man Jett wasn't supposed to be here yet, I can just get a hotel so I'm not bothering you guys."

Wait.

What?

The Christmas party! How had I forgotten the freaking Christmas party?

Since Jett wasn't supposed to be due until a few days after Christmas, Jace and I had planned a party with our friends in our apartment. Park had already planned to visit Becca this year since his parents are off doing some lover's retreat thing in Hawaii for their Christmas vacation. Since he usually crashes with us when he comes to visit her, he was part of the reason we were going to throw a party.

"I'm not sure I'll have the energy to party," I say. With the new baby, it's so hard to remember that we still have a tree at home with presents under it, whimsical Christmas lights strung up all over the place, and stockings over the fireplace. It's as if I've forgotten everything else in my life in the last twenty four hours. "But don't get a hotel. You and Becca should totally stay with us!"

"Are you sure?" Park asks.

I glance at Jace and he nods. "If Mom doesn't mind, I don't mind.

And that is the first time I've been called 'Mom'.

"Of course I don't mind. You guys come and we'll do presents and hang out. It'll be like some sitcom show where the four of us take care of a baby in his first few days of life."

"I'll do everything but change diapers," Park says. Becca hits him. "Okay, fine I'll change diapers."

I laugh. My friends are here. Jett is here. I am skinny again. Everything is going to be perfect.

Right?

CHAPTER 8

Park and Becca laugh from the kitchen as they prepare dinner. We're finally back home and our two best friends are insisting on cooking, which is fine with me. I've taken up residence on our fluffy couch, lying with Jett all bundled up on my chest. He has the most beautiful blue eyes and the softest hair and the most adorable little baby nose.

Jace keeps complaining that I'm stealing too much time from our baby but he can just get over it. Right now he sits on the end of the couch, rubbing my feet that are in his lap while he watches TV. It's almost exactly how we were just two days ago before Jett was born. Something tells me it won't always stay this way. I can almost picture Jett as a two and three-year-old, running around tearing up the place. I can't wait for those days.

But these days are good, too.

We'd had a nice hospital stay and the nurse was right—I needed the sleep. Last night was our first night at home and Jett woke up every two hours on the dot to be fed and I am totally exhausted. Since I'm breastfeeding, Jace can't help me but he did wake up and sit with me until Jett went back to bed.

My grandparents had visited us in the hospital, which was so cool of them to drive all the way from Salt Gap. Grandpa has changed a lot since he first met (and hated) Jace. Now they act like they're old friends.

Jace's parents still haven't been able to fly out from California because of his dad's business work, but they're hoping to be here after the new year. His mom even offered to come stay with us a while if I needed the help. At first I said no, thinking I would be fine.

But now I'm pretty sure that not only do I want the help, I need the help. Babies are hard. Mostly because I've been living like a human zombie for two days, running on an amount of sleep so small I didn't think it'd be possible to still be alive. Maybe I am a zombie. Either way, I am still in love with my life. I never would have imagined in a million years that I'd end up this ridiculously happy.

THE NEXT MORNING, BECCA MAKES US PANCAKES and bacon for breakfast. I sip on orange juice and cuddle Jett while she complains about her community college classes. What she really wants to study (art) is not what freshmen classes entail. I can see why she hates being forced to take math and history and government classes because those are the same stupid classes we took in high school. Unfortunately, until they invent a "only take the classes pertaining to your major" college, we're all screwed. At least she gets to go to college at the moment. I'll be starting a couple years late and that's awkward enough.

But I don't tell her any of this because that's not what a good best friend would do. I listen and enjoy her breakfast and let her vent to me. The boys are gone for a while. Jace had some important client to train and since it was scheduled back when we thought Jett wouldn't be born yet, he had taken the client and their money up front. Jace wanted to cancel and stay home with me, but I insisted that he go. Money is money after all, and Becca and I have things under control here.

"I just can't believe you have a baby now," she says as we settle on the couch for some mega movie watching time. "I mean…we've had nine months to get used to it, but still. You're a *mom*."

"Tell me about it," I say with a laugh. "Life is crazy though."

Jett is sleeping in the bassinet that I've rolled into the living room so I can be near him at all times. He's wearing a tiny little onesie with a t-rex on the front and a little blue beanie on his head to keep him warm. It's pretty cold outside even though we're in Texas.

He is so tiny and fragile and perfect and cute. I love everything about this kid.

Becca gushes about her Christmas with Park and how everything was so romantic it made her want to die. I am really excited for her. How cool is it that my best friend and Jace's best friend have found each other? I know there's a million people who will say that young relationships will never last, but I refuse to believe it. Jace and I are one in a million and Becca and Park can have that, too.

"Unfortunately, I have to head back home so I can get to work on time," Becca says, frowning as she checks the time on her phone. "I was hoping Park would be back so I could tell him bye."

"Just swing by Mixon and tell him before you leave."

She shrugs and shakes her head at the same time, as if the mere idea of going to see him at Jace's work is something she could never, ever, ever do. "I don't think so. I'll just text him."

I throw a couch pillow at her. "You are so weird."

She throws it back at me. "I know."

WITH JETT ASLEEP AGAIN, I GO INTO JACE'S HOME office and power up his computer. It's after six o'clock and his training session was for eight in the morning. He never takes this long on just one client. And he hasn't answered his phone since the last text he sent me.

I check my phone again while I wait for his computer to power up. My last text from Jace said: **Love you, too. See ya'll soon.**

The "ya'll" was me and Jett. It's going to take a while to get used to being part of a duo instead of just a single person now. He sent that text at ten in the morning, over eight hours ago. Where the hell is he?

With the computer running, I feel only slightly guilty for snooping into his stuff. But it's just work stuff and he doesn't keep it password protected so hopefully he'll get over it. I find his scheduling calendar and pull up today's date.

Max training session 8-10

Only two hours are blocked out on the calendar, plus he's only charged for two hours, but what are the chances he really meant eight in the morning until ten at night?

Zero, I realize as I slump down in his computer chair and stare at the screen. Where the hell is he?

Unlike Becca, I'm not afraid to go to his work to see him. But now I have a four day old baby under my care and I don't want to wake him up and load him into my car for no reason other than my own insecurities.

Is that what I am, though? Insecure?

Jace has always been good to me. But still, ideas of him going off to some party to forget all about his wife and kid at home fill my mind no matter how hard I try to push them back away. I know it's totally stupid to even think that. He probably just got caught up at work, which happens all the time.

Of course he's never gone so long without calling and checking in on me and that was before we had a baby. I thought he would be calling twice as much now.

The feeling in the pit of my stomach makes me want to throw up. My first thought is that this is the mother's intuition that everyone talks about—that the sickening feeling of fear filling up my body right now is coming from an awareness that everything is wrong.

But I refuse to believe that. Jace isn't home. There is a reason why.

A loud beep fills the parking lot outside of my apartment. It sounds like a school bus backing up or something, which is really annoying because our apartment is usually a quiet place.

As if on cue, Jett wakes up from all the noise and starts crying. I let out a long breath of air and shut down Jace's computer. I peek in on Jett in his bassinette and his little face is scrunched up and annoyed as his cries turn into sniffling sobs. It looks like I'll get lucky and he'll fall back asleep.

I walk to the window in the living room and pull down the blinds an inch so I can see what's making that awful noise. Hopefully it's not some construction crew settling in for some long, noisy project on the road outside of our complex.

It isn't a crew though, it's just one truck. A tow truck by the looks of it. Jett settles himself back to sleep and I look over at him to make sure he's still lying on his back. When I turn back to the blinds, the tow truck has parked right in the front of our apartment.

That's when I notice the mangled piece of metal resting on the bed of his trailer.

Jace's truck.

CHAPTER 9

Every terrible thought in the world goes through my mind. I'm out of the door, flying down the stairs one second later, leaving the door wide open and my baby in his bassinet. None of that occurs to me though.

I run straight through the grass toward the parking lot, nearly colliding with the tow truck. Jace's truck is hardly recognizable. The license plate on the front is caved in to where I couldn't read it if I tried. The whole front of the vehicle is smashed and mangled, ripped and broken. My mind immediately pictures my husband's body and what would have happened to him in a wreck like that…

The driver of the tow truck sits in the cab, his face glowing from his cell phone. He watches the screen instead of climbing out and even though I can't feel my body, I end up on my toes, banging like a psychopath on the driver's side door.

He rolls down the window. "What the shit is wrong with you, girl?"

"Where's Jace? Where is he? Is he okay?"

Tears stream out of my face. The man gives me an annoyed look followed quickly by one of pity. "Who's Jace? Who are you?"

"Are you serious? The man who owns this truck, that's who Jace is! WHERE IS HE?"

He draws in a deep breath and slowly lets it out, shaking his head as he taps on the steering wheel. "Girl, I don't know anything about that. I was paid to bring this truck here. That's it."

"Who paid you? Where's the driver?" I slam my hand against the shiny blue paint of his door. "I am his wife. Where did he go?"

I refuse to believe any other alternative. Jace is somewhere else. He is not gone forever. He's just temporarily lost.

The man shuffles through some papers and then turns to me, leaning out of the truck door on his elbow. "Look, ma'am. I'm sorry you're upset. There was a collision and I arrived after the scene had been cleared out. I was told to bring this truck to its registered residence and that's here. I don't know anything else."

"Where did the wreck happen?"

"Off I-45, near Mixon."

Every word he says sounds like it's in some kind of vortex. The words make sense but at the same time I'm so hyper focused on one question, is Jace okay, that nothing else seems to matter at all.

Until I hear a baby cry.

I turn back to the man, a sense of urgency like I've never felt before coursing through me. "You have no idea where he is?" I ask in one last ditch effort to find my husband.

He shakes his head. "With a wreck like that, I'd imagine they took him straight to the hospital, girl."

"Right."

I swallow and step backward from his truck. "Well thanks for nothing you asshole."

As I jog back to the apartment, toward the sounds of Jett crying, I realize that what I just said was kind of uncalled for. I don't even know why those words came out of my mouth. All I know is that Jace isn't here and his car is now a paperweight for giants and I am freaking out and oh my God, this isn't happening. There's no way this is happening.

My heart feels like it's being ripped out from the inside. Everything is hazy when I step into the apartment, stumbling toward Jett's bassinet. His little face is red and he's crying with his eyes all squished up. I'm crying too. For a second I have no idea what to do. I don't trust myself to pick him up, not when I feel like I will burst into a thousand tiny pieces any moment now.

I take a deep breath and sink into the couch, rolling the bassinet in front of me. I place a hand on his head in the most comforting way I possibly can, but I know that I have no comfort to give.

Where is Jace? Is he okay? Tell me he's okay.

I check my phone—nothing.

Then I'm dialing Becca. She'll know what to do.

Only she doesn't answer.

I dial Mom even though I know she's on a date with David. No answer.

I pick up Jett and my arms are stronger than I thought they were because he doesn't fall to the floor. I hold him strong and sit on the couch with him. He's hungry.

I feel stupid for not realizing it earlier. Of course he's hungry. While I feed him I try to think of a plan. I can call the hospital, I can ask if Jace is there. I could also try the police department. They would have had to show up to make a report on the wreck. They'd know what happened to Jace.

Surely they can't bury him in the ground without letting his wife know.

I take a shaky breath and burst into tears. I can't think about that. Not now. Jace is not dead. I can't believe it. I refuse to believe it.

Jett's tiny head gets teardrops on it and I wipe them away, but more fall faster than I can keep up with. I can't stop crying. I shouldn't be alone. Jace should be home.

What the hell am I supposed to do?

I call Becca again. No answer. I call Park. Still no answer. They're probably together, making out and loving their life without a damn care in the world that my husband might be a piece of roadkill right now. I hate them. I hate my mother. I hate everyone.

With my teeth gritted, I take care of Jett. I get him a new diaper and a new set of pajamas. I kiss him on the forehead and tell him everything will be okay, even though I'm really trying to convince myself. He looks so peaceful and happy. He has no idea what's going on. I wish I could be like him.

He falls asleep a few seconds later and I head to

the spare bedroom where we keep all the baby stuff I've bought but haven't unpacked yet. I find the massive diaper bag that I planned to use if we took a vacation. I fill it with everything. Diapers, wipes, food, pacifiers, baby clothes. I toss in a box of granola bars and grab some cash from the jar in the kitchen.

Then, I stare at the car seat.

The massive contraption is top of the line. Jace insisted on it. There's a base that fits into the car and this thing is supposed to snap into it. Jace said it would be easy. I'm going to have to trust him.

The car seat weighs a ton and he's just a tiny baby. Man, I've gotten out of shape in the few months I was pregnant. My breathing is ragged as I carry him down the stairs slowly and carefully. I keep picturing myself tripping and sending Jett flying down a set of concrete stairs to his death. I shake the image away and keep walking.

It feels like hours later when I get him to my car. Like magic, the seat snaps into place and doesn't wiggle. Jace is always right about these things. He'd said it would be easy and it was.

Carefully, I hold back my tears long enough to buckle Jett inside the car seat. The straps seem a million times too big for his tiny little body, so I wrap them in a soft blanket to make sure it doesn't hurt him. He stays asleep for the most part.

A fresh set of tears pour out of me as I start my car. Deep down I know I probably shouldn't be driving. Surely my mental state is worse than that of someone who just drank ten margaritas. But no one else will answer their phone and besides, everyone lives too damn far away. I have to get to the hospital *now*.

I wipe the tears out of my eyes and then I put the car in reverse. And I drive.

CHAPTER 10

When I arrive at the hospital a creepy feeling of déjà vu sends a chill up my spine.

Should we go in the emergency room?

I don't know. Is this an emergency?

Just five nights ago I was here with Jace. We were two people, expecting to leave home with a third. Now Jett and I are those two people. And if we don't go home with Jace I don't know what I'll do.

I park in the ER parking lot. Jett sleeps peacefully as I take his car seat out of the base. I drape a blanket over the entire thing and tuck in into the sides. Emergency rooms are full of sick people and I don't want Jett to get those germs. I'm pretty sure that a baby blanket isn't exactly known for being germ proof but it's all I have.

The entire emergency room is empty when I walk in. I glance around at the rows and rows of chairs and find them all empty. A television on the wall blares some news station and a set of kid's toys lies forgotten in the corner. I guess it's not a popular night for emergencies.

The woman at the triage counter barely glances up at me when I walk up to her. Then she notices the car seat I'm carrying and her brows draw together. She reaches for a clipboard of paperwork but I shake my head and open my mouth and try to speak even though it's so dry I fear no words will come out.

"I think my husband is here," I manage to say.

"Name?"

"Jace Adams."

There's no immediate reaction on her face. I had worried that she'd hear Jace's name and her eyes would light up and she'd say something like 'oh, you're here for the morgue, then' and then I'd be so devastated that I'd drop dead right here on the emergency room floor.

But she doesn't say anything for a moment. She

looks at the computer screen in front of her. "Do you know what floor he's on?"

"I'm not even sure he's here." Again, it's a miracle that words are coming out of my mouth. And if they make sense, then it'll be a double miracle. Because the only thing going through my head right now is the constant chant of *please be alive please be alive please be alive.*

"I don't see anyone by that name," she says slowly as she clicks through the computer. "Would it be under another name? When did they call you?"

"No one has called me. I—he got in a wreck, I'm just guessing he might be here, I don't—I don't know." All of the air has been let out of me.

Another nurse in Hello Kitty scrubs with a stethoscope around her neck comes up and nudges the woman. She murmurs something and then widens her eyes as if she's trying to communicate telepathically to the woman.

"Oh." That's all the woman says. Then she turns to me. "Okay so your husband was in a wreck and you're wondering if he's here? No one has called you yet?"

I shake my head. "He didn't come home from work and then a tow truck dumped off his mangled truck and the guy said he was in a wreck near Mixon. No one has told me a damn thing, lady. I'm wondering if he's here. Will you please just tell me if he's here."

She glances at the car seat again and then looks up at me. "Can I have your ID please?"

"What the hell does that matter?" I throw up the one hand that isn't holding the car seat. "Is he here? Is he alive?" Oh God, the tears are coming again. "Just tell me something please."

The Hello Kitty lady nudges the other woman on the shoulder and gives her another eye look. "It's not breaking HIPAA, just do it."

She sighs. "We have one John Doe here. I don't know if it's your husband and I can't tell you anything else. He is alive."

Those last three words almost knock me off my feet. *Thank you. Thank you. Thank you.*

Ugh. And then I'm crying again. But they're tears of mostly happiness, so that's a slight improvement. I clear my throat and smile at the woman. I know that niceness will get me many more places than being a brat will. "Why is he a John Doe? Did he just get here? Can't you find his driver's license and then I can show you mine and prove I'm his wife and then you can let me back to see him?

Please? I'm dying here without knowing if he's okay."

"They couldn't find an ID on him and the last I heard, they can't find a cell phone either. That's not uncommon in car wrecks since phones tend to go flying somewhere or they get broken. We'll get it sorted out it just might take a while."

"Can't you just ask for his social security number or something?"

That's when her face changes. I can tell she's wrestling with herself and if she should tell me or not. Damn those stupid hospital patient privacy acts. Finally, she says, "I'm not certain what's going on, but I think maybe he's unconscious so maybe, I'm not saying that's what it is, but maybe that's why he can't personally identify himself."

The lump in my throat is about to close off my airway. I stare at the floor for a moment. Unconscious isn't the worst thing in the world. He's been knocked out before. He always acts like it's not a big deal. I force myself to smile. "Okay then. Unconscious will be conscious soon enough. I'll just have a seat and wait for him to wake up and ask for me."

Her head tilts to the side. "Well, honey that might take a while. You can leave your name and phone number with me, though and I'll be happy to—"

"No." I walk over to the row of chairs, the same row I sat in last time Jace was in the hospital. "I'll be right here when you need me. I'm not going anywhere."

CHAPTER 11

T*wo Days Later, December 29th*

THE CHRISTMAS DECORATIONS HAVE BEEN TAKEN down, shuffled into boxes and put away for next year. At home, I know the tiny little lights are still strung up around our living room, probably still glowing for all I know. I don't remember turning them off. I don't even remember if I locked the door.

Now, the hospital workers, dressed in black dress pants and a white button up shirt to distinguish them as regular employees and not nurses or doctors take out black and gold banners and stars to hang in the cafeteria. It's almost New Year's Day.

And my husband still hasn't woken up.

I take a plastic tray from the buffet line and fill it up with enough breakfast food for three people. I get muffins and eggs and bacon and two cups of coffee. The woman at the cash register is the same one from the last two days but she doesn't acknowledge me when I hand her my debit card. I guess she doesn't care if hospital guests have to stay multiple days. I probably wouldn't either if I were in her position.

With the food still on the tray, I take it out to the elevator and up to the third floor to Jace's private room. It's right next to the nurses' station so we get prime attention from them.

Jace's mom Julie smiles at me from her position on the recliner in the corner of the room. She's holding Jett, feeding him from a bottle and petting the top of his little baby head. I set the food down on the table and grab the muffin and a cup of coffee. I've never needed coffee more in my life.

"He's such a precious little boy," Julie says. She says it while I'm watching Jace, who is the center of attention in the middle of the room so at first I think she's talking about her son. But when I glance back at her, she's talking to Jett. "He looks so much like Jace did as a baby."

I draw in a deep breath. Yeah I get it. The baby is cute. Why are we still pointing that out? The real situation here, the only thing worth talking about, is the man lying in a coma right in front of me.

After he was identified and I could prove that I was his wife, I mean—am his wife, when I could prove that I AM his wife, I was allowed back to see him. Jace was hit by a drunk driver. As in all cases of irony such as this, the driver, the worthless douchebag who chose to get wasted and then step behind the wheel, walked away without a problem. I've been told that douchebag's Jeep was damaged pretty badly, but that brings me no justice.

Jace suffered three broken ribs, a broken femur, collarbone, wrist, and jaw. All on the left side of his body. The biggest fear—brain damage or internal bleeding—was put to bed after some scans and tests. But he was knocked out so badly that he hasn't woken up yet.

And here's the thing. They won't tell me when he'll wake up.

With all the technology they have today, they can't tell me that one thing.

Jace's dad Gary comes back into the room with a newspaper in his hand. Apparently he has to read them every day even though all of that same information can be found online quicker and for free. He thanks me for the breakfast and dives into the coffee and eggs.

Funny, how the last time I called Jace's mom to tell her he was in the hospital, she'd only laughed and said it wasn't a big surprise to her. This time, I guess the tone of my voice let her know something was wrong before I could even explain it all. They took the first flight here.

My mom and Becca and Park have been visiting often, but not for long because the doctors don't want him to have much company. At first, I had wanted it to be just Jett and me in here with him, but having his parents here have been a real help. Especially with Jett.

I mean, I never wanted to be a bad mother but I'm having a hard time concentrating at the moment. I still feed him most of the time and I change all of his diapers, but I can't really focus on the task. Luckily, I'm not sure anyone has noticed. Julie has been totally in love with Jett since the moment she saw him and she's been begging to play with him so much that I think the situation is mutually beneficial for both of us. She gets lots of time with her grandson, and I get a break.

During my breaks I either go down and get food, go to the bathroom, or do what I'm usually doing—sitting next to Jace. Due to his injuries, they won't let me crawl into bed with him, although I've definitely tried. Instead, I've dragged a chair up as close as possible to the left of the bed where his good side is and then I sit cross-legged in it and lean my head against the mattress.

Jace, my Jace, doesn't look like himself. His head is all swollen and bruised. There's six staples across his scalp and two stitches on his bottom lip. His right side is all mangled and bandaged, casted and stitched. His left arm is almost completely perfect. That's the arm I hold onto, the arm I rest my head on at night.

It's the same hand I hold when we're driving in his truck and I sit in the middle seat.

What am I supposed to do without him?

Every time the dark thoughts of life without Jace slip into my mind, I wonder what I'm supposed to do, how I'm supposed to survive. And the only answer I can come up with? Wishing I could ask Jace. He would know what to do. He would have the right words to say.

But he's not talking.

CHAPTER 12

D*ecember 30*th

"HEY. YOU CAN WAKE UP, YOU KNOW." I SIT UP, glance around the room to make sure we're the only ones in here. We are. Everyone went to get lunch and the only other sound in the room is the steady beeping of the machines hooked up to Jace.

I lean in again, running my fingers across his hair and down the side of his face. "Babe," I whisper. "It's time for you to wake up."

I watch his eyes, expecting a twitch. Then I stare at his lips, all dried and unmoving, hoping that they will form a smile and begin to talk to me.

Nothing happens.

The doctors have said that Jace's injuries will all be healed with time. That it will be months before he's cleared to ride a dirt bike again, but that he should one day be exactly the same as always, minus a few grisly scars. The only thing he has to do now is wake up.

And he's being so freaking stubborn.

I've wasted away many hours at his hospital bed, searching coma stories on the internet and reading about how they think it's good to talk to people in comas because they can probably hear you. And you have to have the hope that they can, right? Otherwise it's just pointless.

I take out my phone and open it to Jace's favorite news app and begin reading him the news. He's always reading the news while he eats breakfast before work so I figure he'll appreciate my effort to keep him informed. "So that McDonald's by our house is gone now," I say, making up the words as I go along because the news app is taking forever to load. "Yep. It burned to the ground. The owner came on the news and said he took it as a sign that Mixon needs more healthy options so instead of rebuilding it, he's going to put in a salad store."

I watch Jace's face for any signs of movement.

But when he's still just as quiet and unmoving as he's been all week, I know he hadn't heard me talking. Jace would be pissed if the McDonald's went away and he hates salads. Good thing I was just making up that story. McDonald's does sound good, though. I've hardly eaten all week but when I do find time to eat, it's something from the café on the first floor. Hospital food isn't as bad as school cafeteria food but it's pretty close. I would kill for a double cheeseburger right about now.

I lean forward, putting my elbows on the bed and resting my phone on Jace's bicep while I read him the actual news. I used to think I couldn't get enough of this boy, of being close to him and near him at all times—but I was wrong. I had no idea how lucky I had it back then. Now I *really* can't get enough of him. Being able to touch someone who doesn't respond in any way takes an emotional toll on a person.

I've never been so worn out in my entire life. From breastfeeding to sleeping on a cot in the middle of a hospital room, cuddling Jett in my arms and waking up every two hours for him, to spending every other second next to Jace watching him and talking to him, my body is worn out. I haven't been drinking water because I've been too afraid to pee and miss out on Jace waking up. I can tell everyone thinks I'm crazy but at this point I really don't give a damn.

Julie sets her knitting down in the chair next to her and gets up, walking over to my side. I've pulled my chair as close to the hospital bed as possible and now Jett is sleeping against my chest as I lean my head on the mattress and watch daytime television on the TV that hangs from the ceiling.

Her arm touches my shoulder and she smiles, but it's that kind of smile that almost looks like she's mad at me. "Bayleigh, do you think you could step into the hallway with me for a minute?"

My eyes get wide and I glance back at Jace, half expecting him to wake him and tell her that he doesn't want me to leave. Of course he doesn't. "Why?" I ask, bringing Jett closer to my body.

"I just wanted to chat." She briefly glances toward the other side of the room where Becca and Park are playing a game of Uno and eating some of the pizza they brought us for lunch. "You know, privately."

"Guys, can you leave for a minute?" I ask my friends.

Jace's mom waves her hand and says, "No, no that's fine. Bayleigh and I will step outside. Y'all can keep eating."

Becca gives me a single look and in that split second I know she's telling me that she will only listen to me. "Go, please," I tell her. They leave the Uno cards on a table and get to up leave, Park taking an extra slice with him for the walk to the hallway.

When we're alone, with the hospital door closed behind him, I glance up at her. "What's up?" I'm not an idiot. I can tell she's concerned about some-thing, maybe even about to yell at me, but I keep my voice light.

She sighs. "Bayleigh, honey. I love you so much and I hope you know that."

"I love you, too," I say, still with the light tone in my voice.

Her lips flatten together and she watches me with the saddest look in her eyes. "Honey, I think you need to go home. Just for a little bit."

I snort.

There's really nothing else to say here.

I turn my attention back to the television. The couple on the screen are getting divorced on daytime television by some creepy guy who doesn't really look like he's a real judge.

"Honey, I'm serious. Will you just hear me out?"

I look at her again, this time with my jaw firmly clenched tight. "Why should I go home? My husband is here."

"Yes he is, and he's in excellent hands. But you haven't showered in over four days. You've been wearing the same clothes. You can't keep using wet napkins to clean up Jett's burbs. You need to go home, take a hot shower and maybe get a real nap. You can even leave Jett with us if you want."

My eyes narrow. "Or of course you can bring him home with you," she says quickly. "We're just concerned about you."

"I'm fine. Becca has been bringing me diapers and clothes for Jett and Jett is fully taken care of," I say, feeling the hot annoying pull of tears filling my eyes.

"Honey it's not Jett we're worried about. It's you."

"You don't need to be worried about me."

"It's not just me," she says, placing a hand on my arm. "Becca actually had this talk with me. They volunteered me to ask you to go home. Becca and Park are even willing to drive you because you probably shouldn't be driving right now."

What am I, some kind of nut case? I am perfectly capable of driving.

Even though I know that Becca and Park and Jace's mom are trying to being helpful and loving, I can't help but feel epically betrayed. Who does that? Talking about me behind my back and then have some kind of intervention to get me to go home. I can't go home.

"I can't go home," I say. "Jace might wake up."

The look on her face tells me that I'm right and she knows it.

So why am I then walked down to Park's truck and driven home by two people who I thought were my best friends?

CHAPTER 13

My hands fold over my chest and I let out an indignant huff of breath for the tenth time in as many minutes. "You two are not my friends," I say.

Becca leans against my shoulder from her place in the middle of Park's truck seat. She grabs my arm and squeezes it. "We are your friends. That's why we're taking care of you."

"I don't need to be taken care of. None of my bones are broken, in case you haven't noticed. I need to be taking care of Jace."

"The hospital is taking care of Jace."

Park, who is usually the talkative energetic one of the group, has been completely silent since we left. I'm starting to think he might actually be on my side but is being held hostage by his girlfriend and his best friend's mom. I glance over at him for confirmation, but he's staring at the road.

My apartment smells old and stale. Like the life has been all sucked out of it and replaced with the air of fifty years ago. As I had suspected, the Christmas lights inside the living room are still on. I walk to the wall where they are plugged in, bend over and yank out the cord, making the room go dark except for some sunlight streaming in through the closed blinds.

When I stand back up again, I start to cry.

"Oh, Bayleigh," Becca says, rushing to my side. She holds my shoulders in her hands but I ignore her. It's not intentionally, I just can't focus on anything right now. My hands cover my face and I drop to my knees on the carpet, tears falling out faster and harder with each second. Becca sits on the floor with me, murmuring nice things that I can't even understand at the moment.

My chest heaves with ragged breaths. It's a struggle to breathe between the crying. Like a tidal wave of grief, my entire broken heart spills out of my eyes and into my hands. Becca holds me close.

I regret what I said in the car. Becca is definitely my friend.

"What am I supposed to do?" I say between sobs. I'm not sure where Park went and at this point, I don't really care.

"You're going to pull yourself together and be strong for Jace." Becca brushes the hair out of my face. "Let's get you a shower and some new clothes and some real food. We'll be back to Jace before he knows you're gone."

I nod. Her idea sounds good. I can do this. I can be strong, just like Jace would have been if he were in my position. He's always strong. Always steady. Always there.

How would I feel if he woke up to find out that his wife, the woman he married and trusted to raise his son, was nothing more than a weak idiot who crumbled under the first sign of pressure?

I take a deep breath, closing my eyes and picturing Jace's smiling face the way it is in my memories before he became scarred from the wreck. And in this very second, I know more than anything else, that I will absolutely not disappoint him.

I stand up and swallow the lump in my throat. Becca's eyes are wide with surprise which she tries very unsuccessfully to hide from me. I look her in the eyes. "Let's do this."

She helps me into the shower, getting the water warm for me and setting out a towel for me to grab when I'm done. I hand her my dirty clothes with a grimace on my face, as if seeing them for the first time right here under the bright bathroom lights. God. They're filthy. I'm filthy.

I glance at my stomach in the mirror again, marveling at how the big round bulge is totally gone. I'm a little thinner than usual as if these last five days have sucked every bit of glow from my skin. I step into the shower and wash myself on autopilot, with shampoo and everything. Just like a normal person would do.

The water from the showerhead splashes over my face and I close my eyes and pretend to be smiling again. I imagine a world where Jace and Jett are on the outside of that door, playing in the living room and waiting for Mom to come out of the shower and join them. Then, with every ounce of energy I have left, I force myself to smile for real.

It almost hurts. But I manage it. I'm smiling. I'm in the shower, all alone, but it's a real smile. I take the lie even further and tell myself that I will one day smile again, in front of people and with Jace by my side. He will wake up, I tell myself. He's going to. Then my smile will be completely for him.

When I'm out of the shower, I dry off and climb into the fresh set of yoga pants and soft black t-shirt that Becca had laid out for me. In times like these I feel that she knows me better than I know myself. I would have picked this exact same outfit. It's soft, it's comforting. It reminds me of home.

Plus I can easily spend another five days wearing it.

I shuffle into the living room with a towel wrapped around my hair. Now I know why I couldn't find the hairdryer—Becca holds it in her hand. She's sitting cross-legged in front of the couch, watching television and holding a hairbrush in her other hand. "Sit," she says, motioning toward the spot in front of her.

"Where's Park?" I ask as I do what she said. I take the towel out of my hair and Becca begins brushing it out. I'm thankful I used conditioner as she rakes the brush through my hair with unre-lenting speed.

"He went to get food," she says. "Real food, not that hospital shit."

I wonder how she thinks takeout food could be any more real than hospital food since it's all the same type of prepared-in-an-industrial-kitchen stuff, but I don't say anything.

We watch the History Channel in silence while Becca blow dries my hair. It feels good to have my hair brushed by someone else and I can feel it relaxing me more than the shower did. I find myself thinking about how Becca is possibly the world's greatest friend and for the thousandth time in my life, I am so grateful for her and I feel like I could never, ever repay her the kind of friendship she's given to me.

When my hair is nearly dry, Park gets back. I'm being held in position by the hair dryer so I can't turn to look at him but the smell of the food he's carrying nearly knocks me over. My stomach instantly growls and it feels like I haven't eaten in months. I pull away from Becca as she brushes my hair.

"What is that? I'm starving."

Park laughs and sets a tray on the kitchen counter. There are no bags of takeout food with him. Just a glass dish covered in foil and another foil-wrapped object that's long and thin. It smells absolutely divine.

"Mrs. Molly's homemade lasagna," he says, pulling off the foil from the dish and sweeping his hand through the air as if he's revealing the prize on a game show. My mouth waters and I rush over to it. Now this is food.

"She made this for us?" I ask in disbelief. Becca moves into the kitchen and takes out some plates and forks. The other foil package is a loaf of cheesy garlic bread. Suddenly I think I could eat the entire thing.

We all fix plates of food and sit down to eat at the kitchen table. There's a different feel in the air as we eat, and I'm guessing it's because I've finally pulled out of my depressed stupor. I credit this solely on the food. Mrs. Fisher, or Molly, as Park calls her, is Jace's boss's wife. She's also my friend Hana's mom. She takes her title as Motocross Mom very seriously and is always there to lend a helping hand to people who need it.

"I have to call Mrs. Fisher and let her know how grateful I am," I say between mouthfuls of my third slice of lasagna. I'm about to gain back all that weight I lost this week and I don't even care.

"That woman is amazing," Becca says. "She's always organizing charity rides and stuff." We all nod in agreement and keep eating.

Soon, I am clean and wearing new clothes and walking around with a full stomach. I feel a lot better. Still broken to the core because Jace isn't back yet, but better. I'll be okay as soon as he wakes up. Still, the nervousness that has been plaguing me ever since I stepped out of the hospital is starting to rise to unprecedented levels.

"We really need to get back to the hospital now," I say, doing my best to sound like a sane, normal person who they should totally believe. "I bet Jett is missing me and I'm missing him."

"He's sleeping," Becca says, holding up her phone. "I've been getting text updates every thirty minutes on the dot."

"Really?" I ask, feeling stupid that I hadn't thought to think of that.

"Yep. We've got this. Both of your boys are sleeping in the hospital and Jace's mom is there taking care of them and you're free to stay here longer if you need."

I shake my head. "It was good getting cleaned up but I can't be home for very long without Jace. It just doesn't feel right."

"Looks like it's time to go," Park says. We grab a few more packages of diapers and switch out Jett's old clothes with some new ones. As we pack I find myself getting really anxious to hold my baby again. It's amazing how something so tiny and precious can change your entire being.

I'm packing a fresh set of baby socks when my phone rings from where I left it in the kitchen. "Bayleigh, hurry!" Becca yells. The socks fall from my hands and I sprint through the hallway and into the kitchen, grabbing the phone as my hip slams into the counter. It's Jace's mom.

"Hello?"

"You need to get here," she says breathlessly. "The doctor thinks he's waking up."

CHAPTER 14

I'm expecting doctors and nurses and a flurry of excitement crowded around Jace's hospital bed when I storm out of the elevators in my mad dash to get to him. But the door is wide open and not a single nurse in the hallway seems to care one bit. I find myself thinking something really stupid, something embarrassingly awful and something that makes me a terrible person.

If he's already awake I'm going to be mad.

Of course that isn't true. If he's awake, I'll be happy. I'll collapse into a pile of happy tears and tell Jace how much I've missed him. But if he's already awake I will be a little upset that I wasn't the first person he saw when he opened his eyes. I can't stand the thought of him wanting me and not finding me.

The steady sounds of Jace's breathing are the first thing I notice when I make it to his room, Park and Becca trailing behind me because they couldn't keep up with my pace. His eyes are closed.

"Well?" I say, turning toward his parents who are playing with Jett instead of watching their son.

"Nothing yet," Julie says.

My purse falls to the floor. All of that rushing for nothing. "Then why did they think he was waking up?"

"Something with his brain waves on the monitor thing," she says, pointing to one of the many machines hooked up to him. "They can tell he's having more brain activity so they don't think he's in a coma anymore. At least not a deep one. Now maybe he's just sleeping."

"Well wake him the hell up!" I rush to his side and grab his good hand, squeezing it as I lace my fingers through his. "Hey, Jace. Wake up."

I say it in the same voice I use when he's slept through his alarm clock and is in danger of being late to work. "Wake up, babe. You're late."

He doesn't do anything. I squeeze his hand a little tighter, hoping the pain will cause him to flinch, if not wake him up completely. Of course that doesn't work. I look over him at the broken bones and stitches and bruises. I doubt me squeezing on his arm will do any good at all.

"Stupid doctors," I mutter under my breath as I carefully climb into bed next to Jace, not caring one bit about hospital safety. This one side of his body is practically unharmed, so I snuggle up against him, resting my head on his chest and arm. The steady rise and fall of his chest feels comforting. I can almost close my eyes and pretend we're back at home, lying in our bed and nothing bad has happened to us.

Almost.

I feed Jett and change his diaper and that's the only time I leave Jace's bed. Luckily only one nurse comes in to check on him and she doesn't say anything. Jett's still so tiny that he fits perfectly between the crook of me and Jace, all snuggled up in his burrito blanket. I hope he knows he's with his mom and dad. He's already spent half of his life without a father.

That night, Jace's parents decide to leave the hospital and go back to their hotel to clean up and have dinner out at a restaurant instead of in the café. For the first time in a long time, neither one of our parents are here and Becca and Park are out as well. We're all alone, just my family and me.

Once Jett is asleep, I tuck him into the bassinet we've brought to the hospital and I go back to sit on Jace's bed.

Now that no one's watching, I can pull out the big guns.

"Okay, Jace Adams. It's time to wake up." My voice is stern and demanding. "Now." I sound like a drill sergeant. I guess it's not good enough.

I lean close to his ear. "Wake up or I'm divorcing you." Lies. All lies. But it doesn't matter anyhow because he's not waking up to question them. I sigh and poke him right in the forehead. "Babe please wake up. This is annoying. This is like seriously the most annoying thing you've ever done."

I'm a little embarrassed to admit this but I poke him in the face a few more times. I try to be annoying, hoping it'll get him to wake up. Then, I lean in close and make sure no one is looking, and I lift up his eyelid. Big mistake.

Seeing his eye roll to the side of his head, completely lifeless and not focused on me brings me to tears again. Every other time I've looked at Jace, he's been looking at me.

This all feels so hopeless.

I didn't want to give up on him, but after feeling like an idiot for talking to someone in a coma for two hours, I ended up turning on the television and looking for something more entertaining than poking my husband's face.

My eyes sting like they want to cry. No tears come though because I think I'm all cried out. I lay back down on his good side, snuggling my head against his bicep and wrapping my arm around his elbow. There's a hitch in his breathing, startling me so hard my body gets cold. Shit. I must have hit something, pulled out an IV or something.

I glance up from where I'm resting my head and for the smallest second, it almost looks like Jace is staring right at me. And then I feel the warm touch of lips pressing to my forehead.

My heart throws itself into my throat and I look up again, this time meeting Jace's eyes for real. All I can do is stare. His lips part slightly and I think he's trying to smile.

His voice is raspy when he says, "Hey."

CHAPTER 15

There's a steady stream of doctors and nurses and friends and family filtering in and out of Jace's room for the next few hours. His doctor says Jace had the best possible outcome because he woke up remembering exactly who he is and what happened to him. Now all he has to do is let his broken bones heal and he will be nearly as good as new.

Then of course, I might beat him up just because he made me worry so much.

My mom ruffles his hair when she stops by in the afternoon. "I'm so glad you're awake," she says, leaning down to kiss his cheek.

"Thanks," Jace says. "Sorry to scare everyone."

"It's not your fault," I say. Jett sleeps in my arms

while I sit cross-legged at the foot of his hospital bed. "Which is really saying something, because if I had to guess why you'd be all broken up and in a coma I'd bet money it would be from a dirt bike."

"Psh," he says, rolling his eyes. Even with bruises on his face he manages to look so confident it's cocky. "I'm Jace Adams. I don't wreck."

"So when do you get to go home?" Mom asks. There's a knock on the door and David and Bentley poke their heads into the room.

"You can come in," I tell them.

Bentley's eyes are wide. "Are you sure?"

"Come on, little dude!" Jace calls. Bentley swings open the door, grinning from ear to ear.

"You look really bad," he says, squishing up his face.

Jace laughs. "I don't feel as bad as I look. Thanks to the morphine."

Bentley doesn't understand the joke. I roll my eyes. It seems like just yesterday my little brother was a baby. He'd cry and take up all of Mom's attention. He made messes everywhere and annoyed the crap out of me. Now he's no longer the youngest person in the family. He's growing up into an awesome dude and a proud uncle. It's weird how life changes so quickly.

. . .

Jace gets released from the hospital the next morning. He has to have a ton of checkup appointments in the coming weeks, but for now, he's all mine. I make a bed for him on our recliner since he needs to sit a certain way until his collarbone heals.

There's no way I could sleep in our bedroom while he's out in the living room, so I use the rest of the blankets on our couch to make it comfortable to sleep on. Jett hangs out in his bassinet next to the coffee table. We pick a movie we haven't watched in a while and I dim the lights. Tonight, the living room is our own little campsite.

I try not to stress out about how I'm now taking care of a baby and a husband. I love both of them and I'll do whatever it takes to keep my family happy. But this is starting to feel like it might be more work than I can handle all by myself.

The baby is hard enough. He wakes up every two to three hours wanting food and needing a diaper change. I haven't slept in days, and that's not even because of Jett. It was from worrying over Jace. Guilt rises in me as I curl up on the couch, pretending to watch the movie.

Am I cut out for this kind of responsibility?

Having a baby wasn't exactly on our agenda, but we knew we'd be able to handle it if we set our mind to it. And raising a newborn is exactly as hard as I had worried it would be. But now I have no one to help me get up in the middle of the night.

"Babe?" Jace's voice startles me. He had been sleeping just a few minutes ago.

I sit up, throwing off the blankets. "Are you okay, babe? What's wrong?"

Jace's head rolls to the side and a smile spreads across his face. "I'm fine. You're the one who has something wrong."

"What?" I ask, doing my best impression of being totally confused. "Nothing is wrong with me."

He snorts. "Something is wrong. You're doing that thing where your foot taps insanely fast."

"I was?" I frown. I hadn't realized I was fidgeting. I put the smile back on my face. "Babe I'm fine. I'm just tired."

"Tired Bayleigh doesn't tap her foot," he says, running a finger down the side of my face. "Tired Bayleigh passes out the second her head hits the pillow and then she snores like crazy."

I shove him lightly so it won't hurt his broken bones. "I do not snore."

"Mhm, sure you don't."

I roll my eyes. "You're annoying."

"You're annoying."

I balk. "Why am I annoying? I'm trying to take care of you, you know."

Jace shakes his head. "You're annoying because something is bothering you and you won't tell me what it is."

I twist the comforter between my fingers, suddenly unable to look my husband in the eye. "I'm just…" Words escape me and I just sit there, kneeling next to the recliner and clenching onto the blanket as if the harder I hold, the better it'll make me feel. It doesn't work though.

Jace watches me for a moment. "You're just scared as hell about all the responsibilities that have been tossed on you."

"No, that's not it," I say.

Jace narrows his eyes at me. "Okay, fine. Maybe that's it. Just a little bit."

"I'm sorry baby. I never meant for this to happen. Like you said, at least it wasn't on a dirt bike. Then I'd really feel like a dick."

"It's not your fault. You could not have prevented that wreck, babe. And I know because I talked to the EMT who brought you to the hospital."

That makes him laugh for whatever reason. His hand grabs mine and he leans over to kiss the top of my head. He winces in pain from the movement and I shove him back into place on the recliner. "Don't hurt yourself," I say with a tisk. I grab his blanket and pull it up over him so he stays warm. "You need to get all healed up as soon as possible," I say, this time smiling for real.

"What's that smile for?" he asks tentatively.

I give him a sinister wink. "Don't think you're getting out of your dad duties while you're all broken. I'm keeping track of how many diapers I change and once you're all better, I'm going to lay my lazy ass on this couch and let you take care of Jett all by yourself."

"That actually sounds far," he says. "When I get mobile again, you and Becca can go have a spa day and I'll take care of Jett for you."

I lift an eyebrow. "A spa day? That doesn't really sound like me. I've never been to a spa."

He shrugs. "There's a first time for everything."

CHAPTER 16

T*hree Months Later*

Becca and I stand awkwardly in the parking lot, facing the tan building in front of us. It's ten in the morning and we're actually a little bit late because I got to sleep in. Sleeping in was a luxury that I hadn't had in a very long time. Now that Jace is walking without crutches or a wheelchair again, he lets me sleep in every single day.

"I'm scared," I say, looking up at the fancy letters on the front of the building. Even from the outside La Bella looked too elegant for someone who was wearing yoga pants and an Avengers tank top.

Becca nods. "I'm scared, too. You're the one who had to practically beg me to get my eyebrows waxed that first time, remember? I'm not cut out for this."

"Me neither." I shake my head and take out my phone, opening a new text to Jace. "I feel like we're not fancy enough for a day in a spa."

I type out a text to him saying the same thing. He responds a moment later.

Jace: If anything, you two women are too good for a spa like that. Park agrees.

I roll my eyes. "Looks like we're going in."

Becca hooks her arm through mine and pushes her sunglasses up on top of her head. "Let's go."

THE SMELL OF GARLIC HITS ME WHEN I GET HOME at the end of the day. Jace has been experimenting with cooking in the last few weeks and he's starting to get pretty good at it. We're no longer one of those families who eats meals from a box or the freezer most of the time. We actually eat real food.

I set my purse on the coffee table and wander into the kitchen, following my nose to the smell of the world's greatest stir-fry on the stove. "Babe! That smells so freaking good, I'm about to eat it right out of the pan."

"You'd probably get sick and die," Jace says with a laugh as he stirs the mixture with a wooden spoon. "This chicken is nowhere near being cooked yet."

"Fine, I'll wait," I say, turning around. "Where's my baby?"

"I'm right here," Jace says with a smile. He leans away from the stove to kiss me. I put my hands on my hips.

"I mean my little baby. Not my grown-up one."

"He's sleeping," Jace says. "Just went down about five minutes ago so we should get to eat together without any interruptions."

I shake my head, striding up behind him as he stands at the stove. I slide my hands around his back, lacing my fingers together around his chest. "I don't know how you get that baby to sleep so easily. You're magic."

"Nah, I just tell him how awesome sleeping is. Tonight I told him the story of how when you grow up and go to work and school all the time you'll be wishing you got to nap. It put him right to sleep."

"I think maybe you just bored him to sleep

instead if instilling your great wisdom into his tiny little mind."

Jace scoffs. "So mean to me! And I've been slaving over a hot stove and everything."

I kiss him right between the shoulder blades, then I turn my head to the side and press my cheek against his back. "Thank you for everything you do for me."

His hand reaches up and covers mine. "How was your spa day?"

I pull away and face him, hovering my hands in the air so he can see my glorious manicure. Seriously, my cuticles have never looked so good.

"Ooh," Jace says jokingly, fawning over my nails.

"You should see them in the sunlight," I say, turning my hand around and admiring the shiny purple polish. "It sparkles like crazy. I almost wrecked my car because I couldn't stop looking at them."

"Seriously?" Jace asks, concern filling his gorgeous face. I roll my eyes.

"No, not like seriously, seriously. They're just really pretty. I can't stop looking at them. And my skin is smoother than Jett's ass." I look him dead in the eye when he laughs. "It's not a joke. They did some peel on my face and I look awesome now."

Jace flips off the stove burner and moves the pan of stir fry over to where he's set out two bowls of rice. He fills our plates with food and I grab two forks from the drawer.

"Those people had the easiest day ever," Jace says as we sit down to eat. "They spent all day pampering you with these silly procedures meant to make people look beautiful but you're already insanely hot so, it was kind of pointless."

I point my fork at him. "Keep saying stuff like that and you're going to get a striptease before bed."

Jace wiggles an eyebrow. "I'm sorry babe, what did you say? I couldn't hear you because I was too busy thinking about how freaking gorgeous you are tonight."

Our eyes meet and a tingle shoots up my entire body. I love every single thing about this man. All the pain and worry and late nights spent freaking out about him—it's all been worth it, for the moments like these.

"I'm really glad I married you," I say.

Jace winks. "Not nearly as glad as I am."

THE SUMMER UNPLUGGED SERIES

Part 1 - Summer Unplugged

Part 2 - Autumn Unlocked

Part 3 - Winter Untold

Part 4 - Spring Unleashed

Part 5 - The Beginning of Forever

Part 6 - Autumn Adventure

Part 7 - Winter Wonderful

Part 8 - The Girl with my Heart

Part 9 - Autumn Awakening

Part 10 - Winter Whirlwind

Part 11 - Unplugged Summer

Don't miss all of the spin-off series:

The Summer Series

The Believe in Love Series

The Team Loco Series

The Love on the Track Series

The Love at the Gym Series

The Summer Unplugged Epilogues

ABOUT THE AUTHOR

Amy Sparling is the *USA Today* bestselling author of books for teens and the teens at heart. She lives on the coast of Texas with her family, her spoiled rotten pets, and a huge pile of books. She graduated with a degree in English and has worked at a bookstore, coffee shop, and a fashion boutique. Her fashion skills aren't the best, but luckily she turned her love of coffee and books into a writing career that means she can work in her pajamas. Her favorite things are coffee, book boyfriends, and Netflix binges.

She started writing her own books in 2010 and now publishes several books a year. She also writes young adult and middle grade novels under the name Cheyanne Young.

Connect with her on at AmySparling.com

www.ingramcontent.com/pod-product-compliance
Lightning Source LLC
Chambersburg PA
CBHW031749150726
47989CB00006B/2651